MIKE HUCKABEE

Can't Wait Till Christmas!

G. P. Putnam's Sons • An Imprint of Penguin Group (USA) Inc.

I dedicate this book to my sister, Pat, without whom there would be no story of unwrapping gifts and playing with toys days before Christmas. While I confess to hatching the scheme, it was her dexterity and surgeon-like precision with tape and gift wrap that provided the cover. When I was but three days old, she tried to feed me potato chips, which could have killed me, but instead only started my insatiable appetite for the crispy little versions of the spud. She once put Bactine in my chicken noodle soup (undoubtedly to protect me from disease), but I forgave her for that as well. Ultimately, I decided that the best way to get even was to become a public figure so she would be bombarded with questions as to why she didn't try harder with the potato chips or the Bactine, and to write a book that busted her out for her complicity in a story of deception and deceit at Christmastime.

For all she has put up with and the fact that she really has been a great older (MUCH older!) sister, I dedicate this book to Pat, with a little reminder that one should be careful what you say and do—your little brother might write books someday!
— M.H.

For Tanei, who supported me every step of the way. — J.H.

G. P. PUTNAM'S SONS
A division of Penguin Young Readers Group. Published by The Penguin Group.
Penguin Group (USA) Inc., 375 Hudson Street, New York, NY 10014, U.S.A.
Penguin Group (Canada), 90 Eglinton Avenue East, Suite 700, Toronto, Ontario M4P 2Y3, Canada (a division of Pearson Penguin Canada Inc.).
Penguin Books Ltd, 80 Strand, London WC2R 0RL, England.
Penguin Ireland, 25 St. Stephen's Green, Dublin 2, Ireland (a division of Penguin Books Ltd.).
Penguin Group (Australia), 250 Camberwell Road, Camberwell, Victoria 3124, Australia (a division of Pearson Australia Group Pty Ltd).
Penguin Books India Pvt Ltd, 11 Community Centre, Panchsheel Park, New Delhi - 110 017, India.
Penguin Group (NZ), 67 Apollo Drive, Rosedale, North Shore 0632, New Zealand (a division of Pearson New Zealand Ltd).
Penguin Books (South Africa) (Pty) Ltd, 24 Sturdee Avenue, Rosebank, Johannesburg 2196, South Africa.
Penguin Books Ltd, Registered Offices: 80 Strand, London WC2R 0RL, England.

Design by Richard Amari. Text set in Mendoza.
The illustrations in this book were done digitally, with scanned samples of pencil, watercolor, and acrylic.
Library of Congress Cataloging-in-Publication Data
Huckabee, Mike, 1955–
Can't wait till Christmas / Mike Huckabee ; illustrated by Jed Henry.   p. cm.
Summary: Mike is so eager to open his Christmas gifts that he convinces his older sister, Pam, to unwrap and play with them in advance, but when Christmas morning arrives, they are unhappy about what they have done. [1. Behavior—Fiction. 2. Family life—Fiction. 3. Gifts—Fiction. 4. Christmas—Fiction. 5. Brothers and sisters—Fiction.]
I. Henry, Jed, ill. II. Title. III. Title: Cannot wait till Christmas. PZ7.H86363Can 2010   [E]—dc22   2010005104
ISBN 978-0-399-25539-7
1 3 5 7 9 10 8 6 4 2

Christmas was Mike's favorite season. He loved making his wish list, decorating the tree, and eating as many Christmas cookies as he wanted.

Mike even had fun trying to be good, but it was hard. Especially when his mom and dad put presents for him and his sister under the tree early—two whole weeks early!

"Mom, how would you like it if I gave you an amazing present but said you couldn't open it for two weeks?" Mike asked.

"I think I could handle that," she answered.

"Well . . . how about if I made you just sit in front of that amazing present and stare at it every day for two weeks?"

"Is that what you do?" asked his mom.

"Yes," said his big sister, Pat. "He does that every year. It's not healthy."

"That's right," said Mike eagerly. "It's not healthy. You should let me open my presents, and that way I won't make myself sick."

"Forget it," said Mom. "I'm pretty sure you'll survive until Christmas. You know, when you wait for something you really want, it makes it even more special when you finally get it."

But Mike wasn't so sure about that. He had been counting down the days until Christmas since July. And at the very top of his wish list was a football. Not just any football—a brown leather J. C. Higgins regulation-size football.

His mom knew it. His dad knew it. His big sister knew it. In fact, anyone who had ever met or even heard of Mike knew it.

And now the pressure was starting to get to Mike. Was he going to get the football? He HAD to.

Mike could tell that most of the presents his parents had put under the tree were things like socks and shirts. But there were a few larger packages and one that looked the exact right shape and size to be a football.

Mike needed to know. He needed to know NOW. Luckily, his parents were at work. There was only one solution.

Mike ran to his sister's room. "Pat," he said breathlessly, "I need you to help me open a Christmas present."

Very calmly, Pat told him he was crazy. "You can't open your presents before Christmas," she said. "That's just wrong. It's like cheating."

"But some of them have *your* name on them, Pat. And they're just sitting there, all lonely and bored. C'mon— isn't there one special present that you've been dreaming about? Don't you want to know if you're going to get it?"

"*You're* the one who's going to get it," she said. But Mike could tell she was curious.

A few minutes later, brother and sister were in front of the tree.

"Now what do we do?" asked Pat.

"Let's see," said Mike. "I count six presents for you and six for me."

"Wow," said Pat. "Mom is REALLY fair."

"Wait," said Mike. "Do you realize it's only twelve days until Christmas, and that we have twelve presents sitting right in front of us? This is FATE! This is our DESTINY! This is the REAL 'Twelve Days of Christmas.'"

"What are you talking about?" said Pat.

Of course, Mike was more than happy to explain his plan. Each day they would open their gifts and play all afternoon. At the end of the day, before their parents got home from work, Pat would rewrap the presents, good as new, and put them right back where they had been.

"This way," Mike said triumphantly, "Christmas will last twelve days instead of just one. Plus we can stop bugging Mom and Dad about letting us open stuff early. I know they'll like that."

"I guess that makes sense," Pat said.

"Of course it does!" said Mike. He picked up a certain package with his name on it and said with a sly smile, "Let's open *this* one first."

Pat examined it closely. "The wrapping paper is very delicate," she said, shaking her head. "And there are only three pieces of tape holding it together. This isn't going to be easy."

"Just open it! Open it!" Mike was having a hard time holding himself together.

"Okay, okay, don't rush me." Pat slid one fingernail between paper and tape. "I think I can slide this baby right out the end," she said.

"Do whatever you have to do," commanded Mike.

Yes! There it was, in all its glory. Brown. Leather. J. C. Higgins. Regulation size. Football.

Mike went berserk. He grabbed the ball. "I got it, I got it, I got it," he screamed, leaping around the living room.

"Hallelujah! Touchdown!"

"Calm down," said his sister as she opened one of her presents. "You better save some of your energy for Christmas morning. We're going to have to act surprised, delighted, and amazed."

"It's a deal," shouted Mike as he ran out the door to play football with his friends.

"It's a deal," said Pat, taking the microscope out of her new chemistry set.

On Christmas morning, Pat poked her brother. "Remember to act surprised!"

Mike quickly put on a big grin. "Oh boy, I can't wait to get started," he said to his parents. They were on the sofa, ready for the big show.

"I just never get tired of seeing our kids so happy on Christmas morning," said Mom with a contented sigh. "It's such a great way to start the day, full of joy and excitement."

"Let me at 'em," shouted Pat, rubbing her hands together.

Wow, thought Mike. She's really good.

Mike was starting to have doubts about his own acting abilities, and suddenly he wasn't feeling very joyful.

His mom handed him the large package.

"Is this what I think it is?" he squeaked.

"Look, honey," Dad said to Mom. "Mike is so excited, his hands are *shaking*."

"Oh my gosh, I can't believe it! It's a J. C. Higgins football! I'm so surprised!" Actually, the only thing that would have surprised Mike at that moment was if the football had leaped up and whacked him on the head.

Pat jumped in, just in the nick of time. "Hey, hey! Look at this chemistry set! It says you can do more than a hundred experiments!"

Mom and Dad leaned in for a closer view of the amazing chemistry set. "Wait a minute, there," said Dad. "Let me see that . . ."

Pat clutched it to her chest. If her dad got any closer, he'd see that half the experiments had already been done.

"What are you doing, Pat? I just want to see that box. It looks like it's been used."

"It's fine!" snapped Pat. "It's perfect! No problems here, Dad."

"Okay, okay. If you say so," he said.

Meanwhile, Mike was busy trying to wipe the mud off his football.

"What are you doing there, Mikey?" asked Mom.

"Oh, I'm, um, I'm just buffing the leather—that's what the pros do."

"Good for you," she said. "Hey, you know what we're missing? Christmas music!" She jumped up, turned on the radio, and began to dance and sing: "On the twelfth day of Christmas, my true love gave to me," she warbled.

Mike was feeling worse and worse. He wondered how his mom would feel if she knew about his version of "The Twelve Days of Christmas." Probably not very good.

Before Mike could think about it any more, his dad picked up his football. "I remember when I got my first . . ." he began. Then he stopped. He stared at the football. He rubbed his fingers across the leather and they came away dirty.

"That's strange," said Dad.

"What are you talking about?" said Mom.

Dad tossed the football to his wife. "I present to you Exhibit A: a muddy football. And over by Pat, Exhibit B: a dirty beaker. Kids, why don't you tell us what's going on here?"

Mike put his head in his hands. In a very small voice he said, "I couldn't wait till Christmas to find out if I was going to get the football. And when I found the package under the tree, I had to open it. I asked Pat to help me. Then we went crazy—we opened all your gifts. We thought it would be fun."

"And was it as much fun as you thought it would be?" asked his mom.

"Well, yes, at first," said Mike. "But now I feel really sad."

"Me too," said Pat.

"I really hate waiting for presents," said Mike, "but I think I hate the way I feel right now even more. I ruined Christmas morning. I'm really sorry."

Mike sniffled a bit. He waited for his parents to tell him what his punishment would be. He wished he could go back and tell his past self to *just be patient*.

"Well, you did ruin Christmas for yourselves, and I guess that's a pretty big punishment all on its own," said Dad. "I know it's hard to do, but you need to remember that Christmas isn't just about presents. It's a time for us to celebrate together. And if you do something sneaky, like open presents ahead of time, that means the real joy in Christmas will disappear. Can you promise to remember that?"

"Yes, Dad," said the two children.

Mike and his sister kept their promise. And when next Christmas rolled around, they opened their presents— and they were surprised and delighted and amazed. And everyone could tell that they weren't faking.